SCR
a
TERRIBLE BEASTIES

For the children I've known, past and present,
at Gillieston Primary School—JG

For my special Katz and kittens—MV

SCRATCH KITTEN
and the
TERRIBLE BEASTIES

JESSICA GREEN • MITCH VANE

LITTLE 🐇 HARE
www.littleharebooks.com

Little Hare Books
8/21 Mary Street, Surry Hills
NSW 2010 AUSTRALIA

www.littleharebooks.com

National Library of Australia
Cataloguing-in-Publication entry

Green, Jessica.

Scratch Kitten and the terrible beasties / Jessica Green ;
illustrator, Mitch Vane.

978 1 921272 95 0 (pbk.)

For primary school age.

Vane, Mitch.

A823.4

Cover design by Lore Foye
Set in 17/24 pt Bembo by Clinton Ellicott
Printed in China by WKT Company Limited

5 4 3 2 1

Contents

How It All Began

Scratch the ship's cat was far from the sea. Just minutes ago he had been inside a basket, on the back of a carriage. But now the basket had fallen off, the lid had burst open and Scratch had tumbled onto the dusty road. Scratch sat up and watched the carriage roll away.

It was taking Samuel, Susannah and

their mother to their farm in the hills. Scratch had almost become a country cat!

He wriggled out of the doll's dress the children had made him wear, then turned and trotted towards the coast.

Far away, the sea sparkled blue and gold. Scratch must hurry if he was to reach the *Great Sardine* in time, because he wanted to be ship's cat aboard that fishing boat.

Scratch scampered along, his magnificent tail high and the pink doll's bonnet bobbing around his ginger ears.

At the wharf, all was racket and bustle, with sailors dragging cargo on and off the waiting ships. But there was no sign of the *Great Sardine*.

Where the ship had been was empty water, and the *Great Sardine* was heading out to the open sea.

'You forgot me!' Scratch yowled, jumping up and down. 'Wait!'

The *Great Sardine* sailed on.

Scratch twitched his whiskers. There was only one thing to do—so without another thought he jumped into the water. He was a strong swimmer. He could catch up! After all, he had once rescued a parrot from a stormy sea.

But when Scratch craned his neck to look about, all he saw was pink. He shook his head, blinked and looked again. Still pink! He swam around in a circle, but that

didn't help. Wherever he looked,
everything was pink. His paw tangled
in something. It felt like a ribbon.

'Help!' he yowled. 'I'm still
wearing that silly bonnet!'

He paddled hard.

'I hope this is the right way,' he
spluttered, 'or I'll never catch the
Great Sardine.'

1.

A Very Odd Ship

Something soft wrapped around Scratch's paddling paws. It felt like a jellyfish was swallowing him whole.

Then Scratch was scooped into the air in a fishing net.

'*Yoowrrch!*' he spluttered.

'Calm down and let me save you!' said a voice.

Scratch stopped wriggling and let a

pair of bony hands free him. The
hands untangled the bonnet and
Scratch saw his rescuer. It was a boy,
younger than the boy on the last
boat. He was thin and pale, with
ragged red hair, and his skin was
sprinkled with freckles. His bony
hands and bare feet stuck out from
patched clothes far too small for him.

Scratch wondered if he had found the *Great Sardine*. But then he realised the boat was too small. Its sides were low, it had a high pointed prow and stern, and it was wide in the middle. There were only two masts instead of three, and four burly men sat on seats attached along the sides of the boat, working the oars.

At the stern was a tiny cabin, but there was no hatchway, and nothing beneath the deck except bilge water. The rest of the boat was packed with sails, barrels, bundles, baskets, lines and nets. It was a fishing boat, all right, but it was the wrong one.

'Hey, wee cat! What're you thinking, swimming in the harbour?' said the boy. 'And wearing a pink bonnet?'

'I missed my boat!' cried Scratch.

'What's that racket, Jock?' barked a gruff voice.

Scratch peered over the boy's shoulder at the stumpy man at the tiller. He was brown and wrinkled with squinting eyes under bushy brows.

Like the men at the oars, he was dressed in grey canvas trousers and a rough jacket. He wore a floppy hat and chunky boots. Scratch guessed he was the captain.

Two of the men turned to see who he was yelling at. One looked like a sheepdog, and the other looked like a sheep with ringlets.

'Get rowing, Shaggy Stu,' the captain barked. 'And you too, Curly McCampbell!'

The men bent to their oars. The captain turned back to Jock.

'What's that you've fished up?' he growled.

Scratch stretched his head forward to say hello.

'A *cat*? What're you doing, bringing a cat on board the *Jaunty Jessie*?' the captain bellowed.

Scratch's damp fur bristled and he growled softly as he shrank against Jock's shoulder. The men ducked their heads and rowed harder.

'Cats can be useful,' Jock mumbled. 'They can help me do my job! If I could just keep him, he could give me a hand, like . . .'

'Cats don't belong on boats, Captain Fergus!' grumbled a sailor with a grumpy face and tattoos on his arms. 'Useless animals.'

'You're right, Angry Angus,' grunted the captain. 'This is a working boat.'

'No place on board for pets,' added
a man in a kilt and tam-o'-shanter.

'I'm not a pet!' miaowed Scratch.
'I've sailed with merchants and
pirates! I've rescued a parrot and
saved a ship from the Ragged Reef!'

Jock covered Scratch's mouth
with his hand. 'He won't be a pet,
Highland Hamish!' he said.
'He'll work with me and . . . and
keep the beasties away!'

At the word 'beasties', Fergus shuddered. The tiller lurched in his hand, the boat pitched and everyone reeled. The oarsmen glared at Jock.

''Tisn't me rocking the boat!' Jock muttered.

'If the moggy can keep the beasties away, it can stay' said Fergus. 'But only if you do your work properly. Else there'll be trouble!'

2.

The Terrible Beasties

Once the *Jaunty Jessie* was out at sea, the men hoisted the sails.

'Time for work, Ginger,' said Jock. 'Our job is to keep the beasties away from Captain Fergus. Fergus is a great sailor and fisherman, but he goes to blubber if he sees a beastie. The beasties know Captain can't stand them, so they creep up on him to make him yell. We can't get rid of them. They're sneaky and tricky. It would have to be a sneaky, tricky fellow to put an end to them!'

'I could be sneaky and tricky,' thought Scratch, 'if I knew what a beastie was.'

Jock took Scratch to the tiller where Captain Fergus stood steering. 'This is our post, Ginger,' he said. 'Next to the captain at all times.'

The sails filled with wind and the boat listed to one side and cut through the swell.

'Hold fast!' said Jock, as the spray flew. 'We're heading north for the herring.'

'This is exciting!' Scratch mewed. He held on tight as the tiny boat pitched up and down. 'Almost more exciting than being a pirate's cat!'

Hamish, Curly and Stu perched along one side of the boat to keep it balanced. Angry Angus manned the mainsheet and kept the sail full.

They had been sailing for a couple of hours and were far from land when Scratch suddenly saw a flicker of twitching whiskers between two baskets. Jock saw it at the same time. He grabbed his stick and jumped to his feet.

'Get away, you filthy bags of fur!' he shouted, banging the stick against the baskets.

Scratch leapt from Jock's shoulder and batted his paw between the baskets. He touched something that gave a surprised squeak. The end of a bald grey tail disappeared into the shadows.

Scratch pounced, his back arched, tail puffed out, ears flattened.

There was a squeaky laugh.
'Did you see it jump, Snotnose?
Warpwhisker?'

'I saw, Fattus Rattus!' replied
another voice.

'*Ha, ha, hee!*' giggled a third. 'We're
going to have fun on this trip!'

Scratch peeped between the baskets

and saw three rats giggling and rolling about on the floor, clutching their fat tummies.

'Who do you think you are?' Scratch mewed.

The fattest rat stood up. 'I am Fattus Rattus, the greatest sea-rat of all!' he said. 'And we are the Rat Pack.'

'I'm Scratch, Ship's Cat,' said
Scratch. 'I've cruised two of the
seven seas and I've sailed with pirates!
I'm here to keep the beasties away
from the captain. But I'll make sure
I get rid of you, too!'

'Beasties *and* us?' said Fattus Rattus.
'That's a big job for a little kitty!'

With another giggle, the rats
scuttled off.

Jock poked his stick into bundles
of nets. 'Where did they go?' he
shouted.

'*Yoo-hoo!*' a voice squeaked.

Scratch looked around. Fattus
Rattus sat on the rail cleaning his
whiskers.

Scratch scrambled across Highland Hamish's lap and leapt for the rat. Hamish yelled and the rat sidled further along the rail. Scratch jumped to Curly McCampbell's shoulders, then to Shaggy Stu's knee.

Fattus Rattus tiptoed along the rail.

Scratch jumped at him, but Fattus Rattus was already on the scaling bench that ran down the middle of the boat. He winked at Scratch, then headed for the stern where Captain Fergus was steering. Jock guarded Fergus, waving his stick.

Scratch leapt to the bench. Fattus Rattus skittered away. Scratch leapt again. He landed on Angry Angus's shoulder.

'Get off, you foul feline!' Angus bellowed.

Fattus Rattus jumped off the bench and ducked under a seat. Scratch bounded after him.

Suddenly there was a terrible howl. The boat lurched, Angus dropped the mainsheet, the sails flapped and the men nearly toppled backwards into the sea. Scratch froze. He had never heard anything so horrible. Was *this* a beastie? He forgot about the rat and climbed onto a seat to look.

Captain Fergus had let go of the tiller. He was hopping from foot to foot, one hand on his mouth and the other pointing at the scaling bench. On the bench was Fattus Rattus.

'Filthy wee beastie!' roared Fergus.

Jock waved his stick. Scratch leapt. He landed on the bench, then slid off as the boat lurched over the next wave. The sailors scrambled to their seats and set their oars to steady the boat. Fattus Rattus disappeared.

'Jock!' Fergus roared. 'By heck, boy, you're in trouble! I thought that cat was supposed to help you!'

'Useless cat for a useless boy,' growled Angry Angus as he struggled with the sails.

A fine ship's cat Scratch felt! And a fine ship's cat he must have looked, falling over and pouncing on thin air. As for the beasties—they were nothing but a pack of rats!

3.

A Beastly Challenge

That night, while Captain Fergus slept, Scratch crouched on the floor beside his berth. He was ready to pounce on the first rat that showed its nose. Jock sat beside him with his stick.

'We must try harder, Ginger!' Jock whispered. 'Especially when Captain's asleep. Else I'll be in terrible trouble.'

Jock and Scratch were the only ones awake. The rudder had been pulled up and the anchor lowered, and the cabin shook with snores.

Scratch sniffed. There was a definite ratty smell coming from outside. His tail twitched as he crept out of the cabin and into the moonlight.

'Here comes the ship's pussycat,' a voice squeaked.

The Rat Pack sat in a row along the ship's rail.

'I am not a pussycat!' hissed Scratch. 'And I *will* catch you! Wait and see!'

'That sounds like a challenge!' squealed Warpwhisker.

'It *is* a challenge!' mewed Scratch.

'Then here's the deal!' squeaked Fattus Rattus. 'You must try to keep us away from the captain. If you fail, you must stand on the scaling bench and say, *I am not a ship's cat. I am just a pussycat!*'

'And if *you* fail—!' yowled Scratch as he leapt at the rat.

The Rat Pack scattered, darting between the barrels under the bench.

Scratch went back inside. Jock was clutching his stick in his thin little fist, muttering about trouble. But his eyelids were drooping and his head was beginning to nod. Scratch gave him a friendly pat to wake him up. He would not let Jock fail in his duty. Jock's eyelids drooped some more and a tiny snore escaped his mouth.

'Poor Jock,' thought Scratch. 'I'll let him dream for a bit, and keep the rats away from Captain Fergus by myself.'

A scuffling sound made Scratch slink to the door. He would catch the beasties by surprise.

He poked his head out of the cabin
and peered around. In the deep
shadows between the barrels he could
see a shiny wet nose. It was Snotnose.

Scratch crept forward, ready to
pounce. He didn't notice Fattus
Rattus and Warpwhisker slip into the
cabin, creep over Jock's sleeping body
and onto Captain Fergus's berth.

As Scratch sneaked towards Snotnose, the other two rats inched towards Fergus. Warpwhisker slithered under the blanket and Fattus Rattus slunk onto the pillow. Warpwhisker gave Fergus's big toe a delicate nibble. Fergus mumbled and turned over.

Fattus Rattus planted a whiskery kiss on Fergus's nose.

Fergus smiled in his sleep. He yawned and opened his eyes. Suddenly the yawn became a howl. His arms thrashed around like windmills.

'Help! *Help!* Beasties in my bed!'

Jock scrambled up and whipped off Fergus's blanket. Scratch raced back inside and jumped onto the bed. But he leapt onto the wrong end. Instead of landing on the rats, he landed on the captain's chest.

'The beasties are attacking me!' bawled Captain Fergus.

'Where?' yowled Scratch, clawing and pouncing. 'I'll get them!'

But the rats were long gone.

'Get off me, you useless animal!' shouted Fergus, pushing Scratch to the floor.

'What's the racket?' grumbled Shaggy Stu from the middle bunk.

'Can't a man get some sleep in this tub?' snarled Angry Angus from the top bunk.

'Jock, you useless lump!' roared Fergus. 'No breakfast for you in the morning! No lunch either! And that goes for your ginger furball, too!'

Scratch crept outside. He felt ashamed. He was supposed to be helping Jock. But the rats were making him look foolish, and now poor Jock would go hungry. Nothing was going to plan.

4.

The Hunt Begins

The next morning the weather blew
up a gale and the *Jaunty Jessie* tossed
about on the waves. The men were
kept busy trimming the sails and
holding the tiller steady. They
grumbled and swore as they climbed
over each other, for their sleepless
night had put them in a foul temper.

Jock and Scratch huddled at
Captain Fergus's feet, trying not to
look hungry. Fergus sat on a stack of
sacks, the big logbook on his knees.
His ink-bottle was wedged between
two barrels. He was busy writing up
the log, but he wasn't too busy to yell
at Scratch and Jock.

'Quit your sulking!' he roared.

'Make yourselves useful and watch for the beasties!'

Jock watched until his eyes ached. He watched the deck, he watched the rails, he watched the barrels and the baskets. Then he watched the sails and the mast and the clouds.

Scratch sat beside him and kept watch too. When he noticed Jock staring at the clouds for too long he patted Jock's hand to bring his mind back to the job.

Suddenly he heard a whisper. 'Seen any *beasties* lately, Puss?'

Fattus Rattus peeped from the top of a nearby barrel, wiggling his whiskers. Scratch hissed, puffed his fur and swished his tail. The rat bared

its yellow teeth. Scratch got up and
inched towards the barrel.

'Come and get me!' Fattus Rattus
teased.

While Scratch stalked Fattus
Rattus, Snotnose and Warpwhisker
crept from behind another barrel and
headed for Captain's ink-bottle.

Scratch crouched, ready to leap.

He planned to land on the lid of the
barrel. Wiggling his tail, he sprang.
But there was no lid! He sailed past
Fattus Rattus and fell to the bottom
of the barrel.

Fattus Rattus ran around the
rim. 'Tricked again, Pussycat!'
he squeaked.

'What're you doing in there, cat?'
said Shaggy Stu as he climbed past.

'Hiding from work?' chortled Angry Angus as he ducked under the swinging boom.

Scratch tried to jump out of the barrel, but the tossing of the boat made it difficult. Again and again he missed his footing and fell back. The men laughed so hard they had to hold their sides.

'Help!' mewed Scratch.

Jock jumped up to rescue Scratch. He stuck his head and shoulders into the barrel, waving his skinny legs in the air.

Suddenly there was a familiar howl. The captain was dancing up and down, shaking his finger.

The logbook had fallen on the deck.

Warpwhisker and Snotnose were dipping their tails into the ink-bottle and brushing inky marks all over Fergus's careful writing.

'Get those beasties off my log!' the captain screeched.

Scratch and Jock jumped at the logbook together. Pages ripped and ink spilled. Jock and Scratch clutched at empty air as the rats escaped again, slipping between two bundles of nets.

The rats giggled and groaned.

'Oh, my guts!' wailed Snotnose.

'I've laughed so hard I won't be able to walk for a week!' screeched Warpwhisker.

Scratch's fur and whiskers drooped with shame. Fattus Rattus was right. He had been tricked . . . again! Captain Fergus would be even angrier, and all because Scratch hadn't kept Jock's mind on the job.

5.

Trapped!

Jock's punishment for ruining the logbook was to sleep on a sack on the floor, instead of taking a turn in one of the bunks. Scratch slept with him to keep him warm and to keep watch.

They sailed north for three days. The further north they went, the colder it got. When the waves got

too big for the little boat, the men
rowed to keep her steady. Meanwhile,
Scratch followed Jock, and Jock never
left the captain's side. He stayed so
close that Fergus sometimes tripped
over him. But even the yells that
followed didn't drive Jock away from
his job. He was determined not to
fail again.

It seemed to be working. The rats didn't show their noses. All Scratch heard were some muffled chuckles and stifled groans, like, 'Ooh, I've strained my tummy muscles!' and, 'I haven't laughed so hard in years!'

The fourth day dawned sunny. Captain Fergus was so pleased with the weather he decided to eat his breakfast out in the open.

'Bring me bread and cheese, boy!' he said. 'I've not had a sit-down meal for days. Make sure I get to eat it in peace!'

Fergus sat on a barrel to eat in the sunshine, and Jock sat beside him with his stick. Scratch sat at Jock's feet. Bits of cheese flew out of Fergus's mouth as he chewed, and crumbs rained onto the deck, onto Jock and into Scratch's fur. Scratch busily cleaned up the mess. Rats loved cheese, and the last thing Scratch wanted was to attract the rats.

But just when Scratch thought he was doing a perfect job, he heard the dreaded sound.

'*Pssst!* Pussycat!'

Scratch glanced up, his whiskers full of crumbs. Warpwhisker was crouching inside a lobster trap propped against the side of the boat. It had sides of cane with narrow spaces between. The opening at the top was like a funnel that got narrower and narrower as it led into the trap.

'I'm safe in here!' quavered Warpwhisker. 'Pussycat can't catch me in the lobster trap!'

'We'll see about that!' mewed Scratch. 'It looks easy to me!'

He shook the crumbs from his whiskers and padded over to the trap. He reached a paw into the cane funnel and groped around.

'*Hee-hee!*' teased the rat. 'You can't catch me!'

Scratch stuck his front leg, and then his head, and then his other leg into the funnel. He squirmed and squeezed inside.

Quick as a wink, Warpwhisker wiggled out through one of the gaps. It was just big enough for a rat.

But the gap was too narrow for
Scratch. 'Bye, Pussykins!' the rat hissed.

Scratch wriggled about. He was
stuck! Trapped like a lobster!

Snotnose jumped onto the top
of the trap. 'Gotcha!' he giggled.
'Foiled by the Rat Pack *again*!'

'*Miiaowww!*' wailed Scratch.

'Ginger!' cried Jock.

'*Aaaarrrgh!*' roared Captain Fergus.

Fattus Rattus and Warpwhisker were scurrying all over the captain's boots, gobbling up crumbs of bread and cheese. Fergus was frozen with panic. Jock jumped at the rats but tripped up Fergus instead. Fergus fell against the lobster traps. The lobster traps rolled along the deck. Scratch tumbled around inside.

'Have you decided to be a lobster,' laughed Shaggy Stu as Scratch rolled past, 'because you realise you're a useless cat?'

Jock helped Fergus to his feet.

'That's it!' Fergus roared. 'Only one more chance for you, Jock, and then you know where you're going!'

'No, no! Not home, please!'
begged Jock.

'Yes, home,' said Fergus. 'And that
cat goes with you!'

Scratch trembled inside the lobster
trap. He couldn't believe he'd been
tricked a third time. And he couldn't
believe he had let Jock down again,
either. He was a useless ship's cat and
he was a useless friend.

It was late in the evening before
Jock rescued him.

6.

The Shimmering Catch

The next day was cold and cloudy again, and the wind blew strong.

Suddenly there was a shout Scratch hadn't heard before.

'*Holla, holla, holla!*' cried Highland Hamish, pointing out to sea.

He had spotted a school of herring. There was a loud cheer as the men got straight to work.

They dragged a net from under the
seats. Scratch mewed with
excitement. Fresh fish! He watched
eagerly as the men tipped the net
over the side.

'Hold the boat steady!' bellowed
Captain Fergus. 'Don't bring the net
in till I give the order!'

As the *Jaunty Jessie* tossed up and
down on the waves, the men tackled

the sails and oars, and Jock scrambled
back and forth to get the scaling
bench ready. Scratch licked his lips
and purred.

Before long the net was full.

'Gently, boys, gently,' Fergus
growled. 'Get her alongside. Don't let
a single fish escape.'

The men hung over the rail.
Scratch drooled and craned his neck.
He couldn't wait to see his first
herring. He was so busy watching,
he didn't notice the rats arrive.

'Why don't *we* help the captain
haul in his catch?' a squeaky voice
cried.

'And earn a feed at Captain's table!'
hissed another.

The Rat Pack slithered across the deck.

'Right, lads, haul it in!' cried Fergus. 'Nice and slow.'

'Jock, look out!' Scratch yowled. 'Rats!'

Jock looked up, saw the rats and darted forward to protect Fergus.

Scratch leaped from the scaling
bench to the boat rail, but the rats
had vanished. So he jumped onto
Shaggy Stu's back, and then onto
Angry Angus and Highland Hamish.
The men were so excited by the
catch they didn't feel the little cat
leaping across their backs.

Scratch spied Fattus Rattus dangling above Captain Fergus's head. He was scrambling along one of the jib sheets that held up the mast.

The men hauled at the net, ready to heave it onto the deck.

'Hold it! Hold it!' Captain Fergus bawled. 'Don't let them spill back into the sea!'

'If we don't let them out soon, the boat will tip!' Angus shouted angrily, 'and we'll *all* fall into the sea!'

The *Jaunty Jessie* was leaning at a very sharp angle. Scratch clung onto Highland Hamish's back with his claws, watching Fattus Rattus dangle above Fergus. The rat waved a paw at Scratch, then reached down to tickle the captain's ear. Scratch leapt. He missed Fattus Rattus but landed on Fergus's head. Fergus yelped and swatted him off. Scratch fell forward into the gleaming, glistening, heaving mass of herring in the net.

Splat! Squelch!

Scratch wriggled and slithered amongst the fish.

'Rowrrmph! Splutt!'

He dug his claws into the first thing he could find. It was Curly McCampbell's arm. Curly howled and dropped his hold on the net.

'Alright, lads! Bring her—!' Fergus shouted.

Fattus Rattus dropped onto Fergus's shoulder.

'*Aaargghh!*' screamed Fergus.

Angus, Hamish and Stu were so
startled they let go of the net. The
splendid, shimmering catch slid back
into the sea.

'Blasted cat! Blasted boy! Blasted
rats!' Fergus roared. 'By golly, Jock,
this time you're sacked! No wages
from now on. But you'll still have to
work your way home!'

Scratch was still hooked to Curly's arm. He let go and dropped to the boards with a squelchy thump, then scuttled to the prow and ducked behind the coils of mooring cables. Jock followed.

'What are we to do, Ginger? whimpered Jock. 'I *can't* go home!

Who's going to feed my ten brothers and sisters if I lose my job?'

Captain Fergus stopped shouting and ordered the men to hoist the sails and keep heading north.

'We're probably too far north already,' growled Angry Angus.

'Aye, thanks to the boy ruining the ship's log!' said Shaggy Stu.

'We haven't taken our bearings since that happened,' added Curly McCampbell, rubbing his scratched arm, 'because of all the cloud!'

'We'll not turn back until we have a boatload of herring!' shouted Fergus. 'And you'd better hope there are plenty of shoals further north, Jock!'

'Aye,' grumbled Angus. 'This is all Jock's fault!'

Scratch flattened his ears miserably. 'No,' he thought. 'It's all *my* fault!'

7.

An Icy Adventure

They struggled north, into icy seas.
The waves became taller, the wind
got colder, and the men got
grumpier. The only good thing was
that the Rat Pack stayed hidden.

'They hate the cold more than I
do,' thought Scratch. 'I hope their
whiskers freeze off!'

Though the rats didn't show their noses, Scratch and Jock stuck to the captain like glue, even in the wind and rain. At times Scratch was so wet and cold, his fur and whiskers froze.

One foggy morning, four days after the fishing disaster, there was another yell from Angus.

At first the men thought Angus
had spotted another shoal of herring.
Or that the rats were teasing the
captain again. But it was neither of
those things.

'Icefloes! Icefloes!' Angus cried.

Captain Fergus scrambled to the
prow. Jock and Scratch scrambled
after him. Scratch perched on the rail
and stared into the fog. All around
them the water was dotted with ice.

'Take the tiller, Curly!' the captain
shouted. 'The rest of you stand ready
with the oars to fend off any floes
that come too close.'

The men were soon sweating with
the effort of pushing the ice away
from the boat. The *Jaunty Jessie*
weaved back and forth, and every
now and then there was a clunk as ice
bumped against the side.

Scratch heard a squeak. Looking over his shoulder he saw the Rat Pack. If Scratch's fur hadn't been frozen, he would have bristled. The rats crept along the rail, heading for the prow. But they weren't looking at Captain Fergus or Jock. They weren't even looking at Scratch. They were staring at the ice.

'What's happening?' cried Fattus Rattus.

'It's ice!' squeaked Snotnose.

'We'll drown!' cried Warpwhisker.

Captain Fergus saw a floe directly ahead. He turned to warn the crew, and saw the rats on the rail.

His mouth opened. For once, nothing came out. He lifted his hand to point at the rats. But they were staring so hard at the ice, they didn't even notice the captain.

'*Rowwrrr!*' Scratch snarled.

Jock jumped. The rats jumped. Captain Fergus jumped back in panic and toppled overboard.

Scratch waited for the splash. But there wasn't one. The rats peered over the side. Jock scrambled to look and stumbled on a bundle of nets. He knocked against Scratch. Scratch lurched forward, barging into the rats. The rats pitched into the sea.

Scratch clung to the rail as he and
Jock looked fearfully into the water.
They expected to see Fergus
drowning in the icy sea. But he
wasn't. He was sitting on the icefloe.
So were the rats.

8.

Scratch Saves the Day

The icefloe drifted slowly away from the *Jaunty Jessie*.

'Save us, Fattus Rattus!' cried Snotnose. 'We're floating away!'

'We're going to freeze!' moaned Warpwhisker.

'Climb into Captain's jacket pockets,' said Fattus Rattus. 'That'll keep us warm.'

Jock tugged at the frozen ropes coiled near his feet. Then, winding the end around a grappling hook, he tossed it onto the floe.

'Grab the rope, Captain,' Jock shouted, 'and haul the floe back to the boat!'

The rats sidled toward Captain Fergus.

Fergus was frozen with fear. All he could do was to stare at the rats.

They sidled closer and closer. Then they clambered along Fergus's leg and headed for the pocket of his jacket.

The icefloe floated further away.

'The rope, Captain!' begged Jock.

'*Aaarrgghh!*' Fergus bellowed. He wriggled out of his jacket and threw it to the edge of the floe.

The rats scrambled clear and scampered back towards the captain.

'Head for his trouser pockets, boys!' shouted Fattus Rattus.

'Get away from my captain, you horrible ratbags!' Scratch yowled.

He ran along the rail, made a flying leap for the icefloe and sailed through the air.

The rats stopped to stare.

'The *rope*, Captain!' Scratch yowled, as he scrabbled for a hold on the edge of the ice.

Fergus gaped from the rats to Scratch and back again.

'Captain overboard!' yelled Jock.

The crew dropped their oars and jostled to the prow.

'Grab the rope!' roared Shaggy Stu.

At last Fergus came to his senses. He grabbed the rope and wedged the grappling hook into the ice. While he pulled on one end, the men pulled on the other, and Scratch kept the rats at bay.

The icefloe finally bumped against the boat. The first thing Captain Fergus did was scoop up Scratch and hand him to Jock. Then many hands reached out to haul the captain back on board.

The rats crowded to the edge of the ice.

'I wouldn't try climbing up that rope,' Scratch mewed. 'This boat has had enough of your pranks. You made the captain fall overboard!'

'It was an accident!' cried Fattus Rattus. 'We were just looking at the ice!'

'And you got Jock and me into terrible trouble!' yowled Scratch. 'Your jokes got us sacked.'

The icefloe began to drift away.

'Please, cat!' begged Fattus Rattus.

'Keep your eyes peeled for a boat whose captain doesn't mind rats!' said Scratch. 'There's bound to be one along soon.'

The rats trooped sadly across the floe to Fergus's jacket. Snotnose dived up one of the sleeves. Warpwhisker followed him.

'Think about your challenge,' mewed Scratch. 'Maybe I should make you say, *We are not a Rat Pack. We are just house mouses*! I hope you learn a lesson and are kinder to your next captain.'

'We'll meet again, Puss,' Fattus Rattus squealed. 'You wait and see!'

Then he too disappeared up the sleeve of the captain's jacket. The last Scratch saw of him was his scaly grey tail.

How It All Ended

Scratch sat on the prow of the *Jaunty Jessie* and purred happily. His tummy was stuffed with herring and his fur gleamed. Everything had worked out perfectly. After his adventure on the ice, captain Fergus had decided that northern waters were too wild for him.

They had turned around, sailed south, caught a boatload of herring, and were heading into port.

Best of all, Jock wasn't being sent home. He had saved Captain Fergus from the beasties *and* from the ice, and was to be made a real crew member, starting as Lookout. Fergus was pleased with Scratch, too, so he was allowed to stay on as ship's cat.

Now, as the men eased the little boat towards the quay, they passed a ship lying at anchor. Scratch gazed up at the vessel towering above the *Jaunty Jessie*. The sailors patrolling its deck were clean and spruce in their maroon uniforms, and the pink paintwork glistened in the sun.

Scratch had never seen a pink ship.

'What sort of cat would a ship like
that have?' Scratch wondered to
himself. 'A lady cat? Or a fluffy cat?
Or even a pink one?'

He craned upwards, searching for
a cat. There was no cat on the rails,
and no cat on the bridge, and no cat
on the spars or yardarms.

'Maybe a pink ship
doesn't need a cat,' Scratch thought.

Then he saw something perched
high on the pink ship's bow.

'*Prrrp!* What's that?' Scratch
mewed.

It was a bundle of striped fur.
Scratch looked closer and saw it was a
big ginger cat.

'That doesn't look the right kind of cat for a pink ship,' he thought. 'A cat with tattered ears, bristling whiskers, ragged fur and three legs!'

Three legs!

'Meeeowwch!'

Three legs! Ginger fur! It couldn't be!

'Paa?' Scratch mewed. *'Paaaa!'*

The big cat turned and looked down at the ginger kitten. 'Are you . . . you're one of *mine*!' he growled. 'What are you doing at sea?'

Scratch jumped up and down on *Jaunty Jessie*'s rail. 'Look at me!' he mewed proudly. 'I'm just like you! I'm a ship's cat, too!'

'Well, barnacles and bowsprits, so you are!' said Paa.

Scratch was so proud he could hardly keep still. But he did. He held on tight with his magnificent tail in the air, and as the *Jaunty Jessie* sailed past, he was sure he saw his Paa raise his own tail in salute!

Words Sailors Use

aloft	above the deck of the ship, perhaps in the rigging
barnacles	small shellfish found stuck to the bottoms of ships
berth	a shelf-like sleeping space on a ship
bilge water	dirty water collected below the deck of a ship
boom	a long pole used to extend the bottom of a ship's sail
bow	the front part of a ship
bowsprit	a large pole that sticks out from the front of a ship
bridge	a raised platform where the sailor in charge nagivates the ship
cargo	the goods that a ship carries
grappling hook	a metal object with hooks, used to grip onto things
herring	an edible fish that lives in shoals
jib sheet	the rope that controls a triangular sail
lie at anchor	when the ship is held still by the anchor
logbook	book used to record how far a ship has travelled

Lookout	sailor who watches out for approaching hazards, other ships or land
mainsheet	the rope that controls the mainsail
mast	a stout pole rising straight up from the deck of a ship, which supports the yards and sails
mooring cables	cables used to secure a ship in a particular place
prow	the front part of a ship which is above the waterline
quay	a place for ships to load or unload their cargoes
rudder	a wooden board found under the ship's stern, used for steering
shoal	a group of fish
spar	a stout pole used on a ship as a mast, yard, or boom
stern	the rear part of a ship
swell	long, unbroken waves
take a ship's bearings	use a compass and a map to find a ship's position in the ocean
tiller	a wooden bar used to turn the rudder
trim the sails	adjust the sails
wharf	a harbourside pier, by which ships are moored
yardarm	either end of the pole at the top of a square sail

About the Author

Jessica Green has always loved cats, and shares her home with four furry feline friends—Fang, Felis, Tre and Tumnus.

About the Artist

Mitch Vane would love to run away to sea but she can't because after half an hour on a boat she gets seasick!

Acknowledgements

Thanks to Michael, for trying, and failing,
to teach me to love the water.

Thanks to Nick, Richard and Gillian,
for assuring me that writing about mad
kittens is far more useful than a tidy house.

Thanks to Mitch, for seeing Scratch
so clearly.

Special thanks to Margrete, for planting the
idea of Scratch into my mind.

Jessica

For more exciting action with
the swashbuckling

SCRATCH KITTEN

look out for his other adventures ...

SCRATCH KITTEN
GOES TO SEA

SCRATCH KITTEN
on the
PIRATE'S SHOULDER

SCRATCH KITTEN
and the
RAGGED REEF

SCRATCH KITTEN
and the
TREASURE ISLAND

SCRATCH KITTEN
and the
GHOST SHIP